# Thank You, Pooh!

Pooh

### By Ronne Randall
### Illustrated by Rigol

## A GOLDEN BOOK · NEW YORK
Golden Books Publishing Company, Inc., Racine, Wisconsin 53404

One day Pooh got some new honey pots.
"Well, now I'll have to give some old honey pots
away to make room for the new ones," he said.

Pooh put ten empty honey pots in his
wagon and went to Piglet's house.

"Good morning, Piglet!" said Pooh. "I wonder, do you need a honey pot?"

"No," said Piglet, "what I really need is a new stool. Look!"

"I have just the thing," said Pooh.

When Pooh turned over a honey pot, it made
a perfect stool!
"Thank you, Pooh!" said Piglet.

Now Pooh had nine honey pots. He made his way to Rabbit's house.

"Hello, Rabbit!" said Pooh. "Do you need any honey pots?"

"Honey pots?" said Rabbit. "No, but I would
like something to hold all these carrots."
"Then some honey pots might be what you
need," said Pooh.

Pooh gave Rabbit four honey pots to hold the carrots.

"Well, it seems I did need them, after all," said Rabbit. "Thank you, Pooh!"

With five honey pots in his wagon, Pooh went to Owl's house.

"Oh, dear!" cried Owl.
"What's wrong?" asked Pooh.

"My books won't stay on the shelf!" Owl said.
"What am I to do?"

Pooh put two honey pots on the shelf.
"Honey pot bookends!" cried Owl. "What a
good idea!"

Pooh had three honey pots left. He met Tigger and Roo carrying two big bunches of flowers. "They're for Mama," Roo told Pooh.

"Surprise!" said Tigger when he saw Kanga.

"We picked these flowers just for you,"
Roo said to his mother.

"Oh, thank you, dears," said Kanga. "They are
beautiful. But what shall I put the flowers in?"

"Honey pots make perfect vases," said Pooh.
"Why, thank you, Pooh!" said Kanga.

"Oh, bother! One honey pot left," said Pooh. "Who can I give it to?"

Just then he saw a honey tree!

"I know," Pooh said. "I'll give it to—me! After all, the *best* thing to do with a honey pot is . . .

fill it with honey!"